THE NIGHT IS

LIKE AN ANIMAL

CANDACE WHITMAN

Farrar   Straus   Giroux
New York

For Katie, Elizabeth, and Claire

Published simultaneously in Canada by HarperCollins*CanadaLtd*
Color separations by Hong Kong Scanner Arts
Printed and bound in the United States of America by Worzalla
Designed by Lilian Rosenstreich
First edition, 1995

Library of Congress Cataloging-in-Publication Data
Whitman, Candace.
The night is like an animal / Candace Whitman. — 1st ed.
        p.   cm.
[1. Night—Fiction.   2. Stories in rhyme.]   I. Title.
PZ8.3.W6114Ni 1995 [E]—dc20 94-44359 CIP AC

The Night is like an animal
that nibbles on the day.

Everywhere it takes a bite

the sky turns dark and gray.

Night eats until the day is done,

then breathes a happy sigh—

which starts the evening breezes,

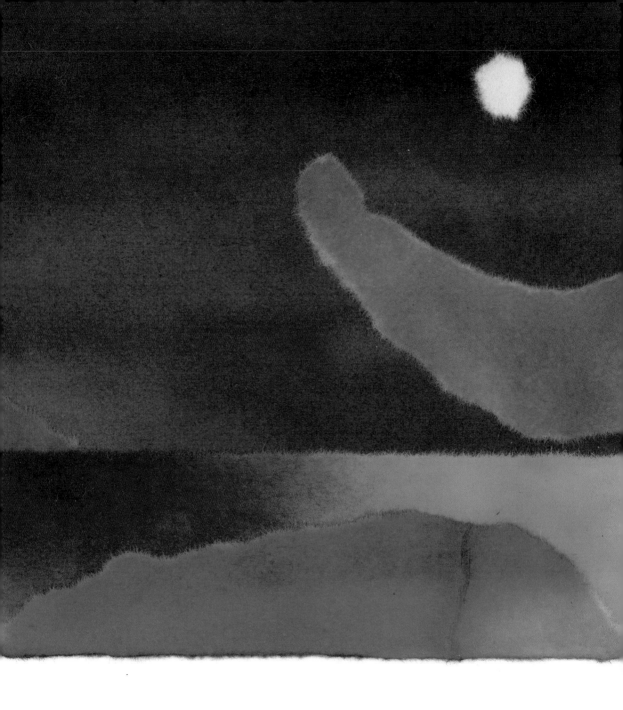

and blows the moon up high.

Turning round to quench its thirst,

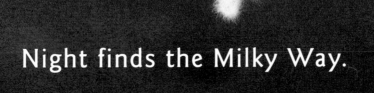

Night finds the Milky Way.

It laps a little milk before

coming

    back

        down

            to

                stay.

Upon the quiet land
Night's fur is soft and black.

Its paws stretch over half the earth
with heaven on its back.

Night curls itself around the dreams

of children as they sleep.

Safe in Night's embrace,
their rest is sweet and long and deep.

Just before they wake up,

Night moves upon all fours—

its bushy tail bobs gently
as it slips past bedroom doors.

Out on the horizon,

Night runs away from dawn,

its paw prints hid in shadows
upon the morning lawn.